For Louise.

P. J.

And...

Philippe Jalbert

BERBAY
PUBLISHING

No!

Don't touch the butterfly!

If you do, it will fly away

and...

the butterfly will make a flower petal fall

and...

the petal will fall on a dung beetle that

will lose its ball of dung

and...

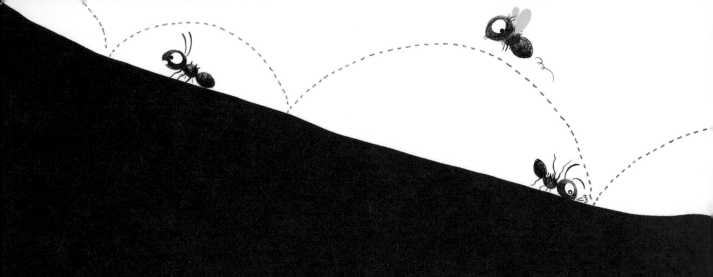

the dung ball

will fall into a river

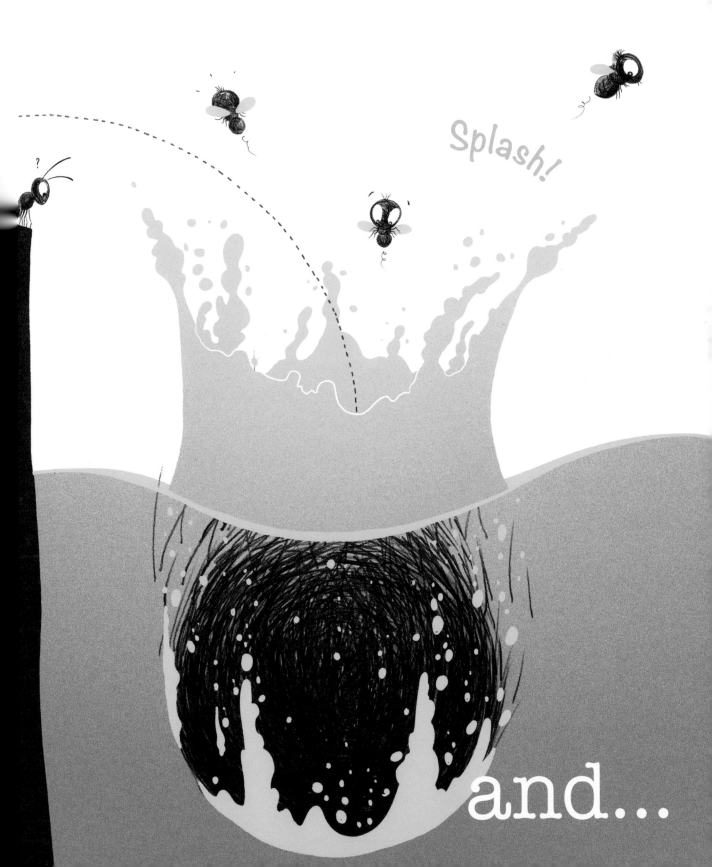

the ball will block up the water, which will rise and rise and rise

until it forces the dam wall to give way

and...

the water will flood into the tunnel of a mole that will wake up

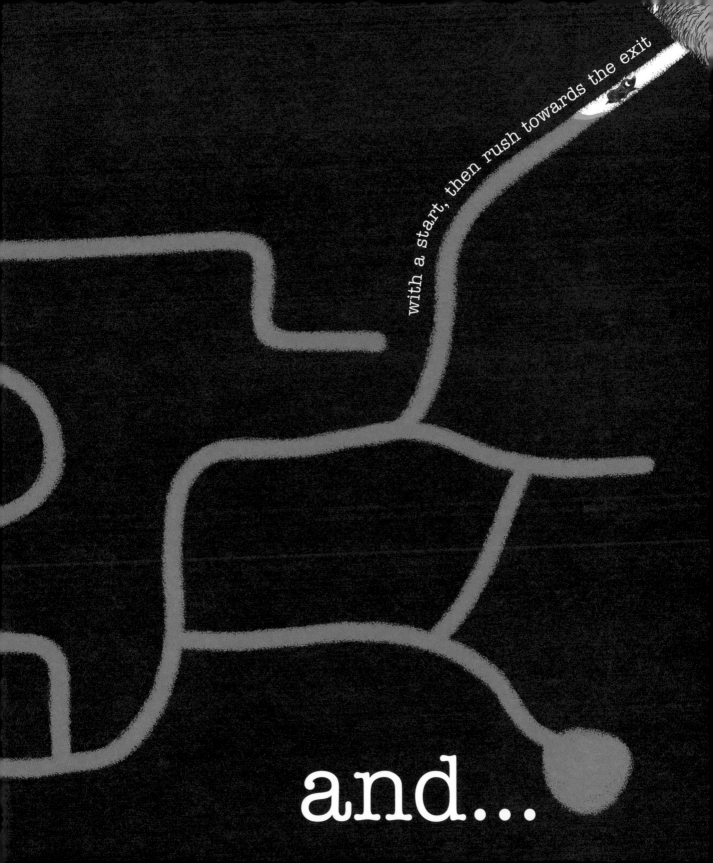

with a start, then rush towards the exit

and...

the exit will be blocked by a clump of fur that

the mole will sink its teeth into

and...

the clump of fur that the mole sank its teeth into

will belong to the butt of a bear that,

rudely awakened from its afternoon nap,

will hightail it out of there

and...

BADABOUM CIRCUS

still half asleep,
will crash head on into a circus caravan
coming around a bend in the road

and...

the mole, the bear and the caravan will come

crashing down the slope, carrying along

with them everything in their way:

rocks,

trees,

cars,

houses,

buildings,

STOP!

I promise

I won't touch the butterfly,

and...

this flower is for you...

Published in 2021 by Berbay Publishing Pty Ltd
PO Box 133
Kew East VIC 3102
Australia

Text and illustrations © Philippe Jalbert
Originally published in French as Et... by Gautier Languereau,
an imprint of Hachette Livre, 2018
English translation by Michael Sedunary, 2021
English translation © Berbay Publishing, 2021

This book was generously funded by the Sidney Myer Fund.

SIDNEY MYER FUND

Printed by Everbest Printing in China

ISBN 978-0-6489533-7-1

Visit our catalogue at www.berbaybooks.com